Fables from the Sea

Fables from the Sea

Leslie Ann Hayashi

Illustrated by

Kathleen Wong Bishop

A KOLOWALU BOOK
University of Hawai'i Press
HONOLULU

For Justin and Taylor, my sons, who provide endless inspiration;
For Alan, my husband, who provides endless love and support; and
For Kath, my friend, who provides endless creativity and friendship.
—Les

To my parents, Kai Fong and Dorothy Wong, who have
surrounded me with oceans of love.
—Kathy

© 2000 University of Hawai'i Press
All rights reserved
Printed in China
08 09 10 11 12 13   8 7 6 5 4 3

Library of Congress Cataloging-in-Publication Data
Hayashi, Leslie Ann
Fables from the sea / Leslie Ann Hayashi ; illustrated by Kathleen Wong Bishop
p.   cm.
"A Kolowalu book."
Summary: A collection of fables featuring a variety of sea creatures found in Hawaiian waters.
ISBN 978-0-8248-2224-8 (cloth : alk. paper)
1. Fables. 2. Children's stories, American. [1. Zoology—Hawaii—Fiction. Fables.
3. Short stories.] I. Bishop, Kathleen Wong, ill. II. Title.
PZ8.2H35 Fae 2000
[Fic]—dc21   99-057299

University of Hawai'i Press books are printed on
acid-free paper and meet the guidelines for permanence
and durability of the Council on Library Resources.

Printed by C & C Offset Printing Co., Ltd.

Contents

The Moray Eel and the Little Shrimp

Sunlight drizzled through the water, falling gently upon a rocky reef. A speckled moray eel waited patiently for supper to swim by her cave. With her sharp teeth and speed, she soon caught a small fish.

Nearby, a little red-and-white banded shrimp foraged for food. *He's hungry,* the moray thought as she dropped the last bite of her meal in his direction. Grabbing the food with one pincer, the shrimp waved his thanks with another. The moray disappeared back into her home.

Months later, the little shrimp recognized the same moray eel rubbing herself carefully against the jagged coral.

"Oh, this terrible itch," moaned the moray eel. The rubbing helped for a while, and then the maddening itch returned. If she scraped any harder, the coral would bite into her soft flesh. Which was worse—the pain or the itch?

The shrimp edged closer. As the poor moray eel twisted in agony, she exposed sharp teeth that could crush a small shrimp instantly. Despite his fear, the tiny shrimp couldn't bear to see the moray eel suffer.

Cautiously approaching the writhing moray,
he bowed low. "Perhaps I can help."

"How can you help me? You are very little and this itch is very big!"
groaned the poor moray eel.

"I can eat the parasites that cause the itch." The shrimp demonstrated by
waving and snapping his three sets of pincers.

"Really? You can do that?" the moray asked, astounded. "Why would
you do that for me?"

"Once you gave me food. Now you're in great distress and I would like to
repay your kindness."

"Well, that's very generous of you."

"I ask only one thing in return."

"What's that, little one?" The moray eel leaned closer toward the shrimp.

"Please don't eat me."

"Oh, I can do more than that. All your meals are on me!" Throwing back her
head, the moray laughed, tickled by her own joke.

From that day on, the tiny red-and-white shrimp and the moray eel traveled
through the maze of coral caves together. The little shrimp never knew
hunger, and the moray eel never had another itch.

***An act of kindness, no matter how small,
should never be forgotten.***

The 'Iwa's Theft

Timing is everything, thought the 'iwa, waiting for just the right moment. A gray-brown seabird rose above the foamy waves with her catch wriggling in her mouth.

"Now!" yelled the 'iwa as he charged the shearwater, his slender black wings angled into a diving position. Startled, the bird dropped her catch. Before she could recover, the 'iwa had already swooped down and retrieved the fish in midair.

"That was perfect!" exclaimed the 'iwa happily. Flying away with the fish in his bill, he turned his back on the loud, angry cries of the shearwater.

"Thief! Stop, thief!"

But the 'iwa paid no attention to the furious shearwater.

The next day, the 'iwa waited for a different bird to catch a meal. This time it was a red-footed booby, the 'iwa's favorite food provider.

"Ah, lunch is ready. Here I go." The 'iwa zoomed toward the booby. "I'm a dive bomber! Lock on target!"

Caught off guard by the rush of the wind, the bird opened his mouth, letting go of his catch.

"Thank you!" shouted the 'iwa as he dove by, retrieving the falling fish.

"Hey, come back here! That fish was mine. You robbed me!" the booby yelled, alerting the other birds to the 'iwa's presence.

But it was too late; the 'iwa had already left with the booby's catch.

In time, the 'iwa settled down to raise a family. With his speed and accuracy, he continued to steal from the shearwaters and the boobies to feed his growing family. The skies continued to be filled with his victims' cries of anguish.

"Why do you steal?" the shearwaters and boobies demanded. "What about our own children who go hungry when you take their food?"

Soaring high, the 'iwa ignored these questions. He had what he wanted.

One morning when the 'iwa returned to the nest with his latest theft, his young daughter asked a question: "Daddy, the other children say we are thieves. It's not true, is it?"

The 'iwa hesitated. What could he say? Admit he was a thief and bring shame to his family? Unable to answer, the 'iwa flew off to think. As he soared high above the ocean, the 'iwa watched the shearwaters and boobies catch their food, returning home to their nests to feed their families. As he drifted on the wind, the 'iwa realized he had been wrong to take from the others. What at first had been a game was no longer fun.

From that day forward, the 'iwa relied on his own excellent diving skills to catch food and never bothered the shearwaters or boobies again.

When we steal from others, we rob ourselves.

The Impolite Hermit Crab

Where the golden sand and emerald sea meet there lived a mother hermit crab and her four young children.

"Good morning, children."

"Good morning, Mother," replied the three oldest crabs. The youngest one fiddled with his claws.

"Junior! Please pay attention! It's polite to listen when someone is speaking."

The young crab stopped for a moment and looked up apologetically. "Yes, Mommy."

"Now, listen closely, children. Today we're going to find new homes. Unlike other crabs, we don't have our own hard shells," the mother crab began. "As we grow, we need to find new homes. When we're out of the shell, we're in great danger; we are **vul-ner-a-ble**. That's why you must remember to find a new home as quickly as possible."

Just then a school of buttery yellow trumpetfish swam lazily by, diverting Junior's attention. He wondered how they ate, since their mouths were so narrow. Could they swallow a large sea cucumber? He himself was always hungry. Even now, the thought of a delicious shorefish made him wonder when it would be lunchtime.

"Once you find a shell," the mother crab continued, "check to see if it's empty or **un-in-hab-i-ted**. Knock politely. If there's no answer, probe it with your antennae. Then gently lift it and turn it upside down, like this." Grasping an empty shell firmly between her two claws, she demonstrated with a quick flourish.

Junior's attention drifted to the pink and green sea anemones swaying gracefully in the current. What exquisite dancers! He was mesmerized by their synchronized movements, the blending of their colors, and their never-ending swirling motions.

"Ready, children? Remember what I've taught you and you'll have no trouble finding a new home."

"Yes, Mother," the young crabs chorused together. All except Junior, who by now was busy tossing a clump of drifting seaweed from one claw to the other.

"Off you go!"

Excited, the crabs scurried in four different directions. The first three soon found shells. Each one of them knocked politely on the outside.

"Hello! Is anyone home?"

Hearing no answer, they poked their antennae into the shells and then gently turned them upside down, just like their mother had shown them. Satisfied the new shells were empty, they discarded their old ones. Then they backed in quickly and settled happily into their new homes.

Junior scuttled over rows of finger coral in his search, repeating his mother's instruction: "I must find a new home right away!"

Suddenly Junior spied a beautiful brown and white shell just the right size.

"I'm in luck! There's my new home!" Rushing into the shell, the crab suddenly found himself stuck fast to the owner, an elderly mollusk.

"Oh my!" Junior exclaimed. "I'm so sorry. I thought the shell was empty. Ow! **Oooh**, that hurts! I'm stuck! Mother, help!"

Hearing Junior's cries, his mother rushed over. After much pulling and pushing, the mother crab finally freed the little crab from the shell's owner, who was quite upset.

"Young crabs nowadays are so rude," grumbled the old mollusk.

"Junior! What do you say to Mr. Mollusk?"

"I'm very sorry, sir," apologized Junior, rubbing his sore backside. "I'm really *very* sorry."

"Junior, did you remember your manners?" his mother asked sternly.

"No, Mother, I didn't," Junior replied meekly, his head hanging low.

"Before entering a shell, you must knock politely to see if it's empty."

"Yes, Mother."

"Now, go look for another shell and remember—"

"Yes, Mother, I will!"

This time Junior remembered exactly what his mother had told him and soon found the perfect new home. From then on, whenever Junior searched for a new shell, he never forgot his manners!

If you're polite, you'll avoid sticky situations.

15

The Dreaded Manta

"Watch out for the giant devilfish! They lock their horns on you and then devour you," a nautilus cautioned her niece. She pointed to the mantas' ominous shapes sweeping by overhead. "Don't get too close or the mantas will sting you with their long tails!"

"How do we know they'll hurt us, Auntie?" the young nautilus asked, curious while huddling closer to her aunt.

"Stories are told of how they wrap their massive wings around you and crush your shell! There's no escaping the silent, swift mantas."

The young nautilus shivered at the thought of being stung or crushed. The mantas swam much faster than she could. Even if she pulled herself and all her many tentacles completely into her shell, she wouldn't be able to escape.

Yet, the little nautilus couldn't help wondering about these magnificent creatures gliding serenely in the dark shadows. Were mantas terrible monsters, destroying all who swam before them? Perhaps the well-traveled triggerfishes knew, thought the nautilus, swimming over to them.

"All we can tell you is beware of the mantas! They are very dangerous! That's what we've been told," the fishes replied, shaking their heads slowly.

The nautilus turned to ask the fleet of Portuguese man-of-war but they quivered at the very thought of the mighty mantas.

"S–s–s–stay clear of them. They are s–s–s–so large they could easily kill you. That's–s–s what we understand," they answered, their long blue tentacles trembling.

As she swam away, the little nautilus realized the only way to know the truth would be to find out for herself.

One night while she was feeding, the nautilus saw the outline of a large manta in the shadows not far below. Its immense wingspan had to be over twenty feet. She watched the manta move swiftly through the dark waters, coming closer and closer, its horns pointed directly at her!

Should she flee? The little nautilus shook her head and took a deep breath. Realizing this was her opportunity to learn the truth, the nautilus propelled herself deeper.

As the manta approached, she could see what others thought were "horns" were simply paddles used to guide food into its mouth. Shaped like an elongated diamond, the manta floated leisurely upward. Its "stinger" was only a tail, trailing gracefully behind like the tail on a kite.

Overcoming her own fear, the nautilus reached out with her tentacles to touch the manta as it swept by. The manta's skin was soft and smooth, almost creamy.

The manta circled slowly around the nautilus, displaying its black topside then its silvery white underside. She held her breath again as she felt herself lifted by the large waves created by the manta. Now she was completely enveloped in its great wings!

The nautilus reached out again, this time to stroke the giant creature. The manta circled around again.

Why, the manta enjoys my touch! the little nautilus suddenly realized. Caressing its great wings, she floated happily next to her new friend. Now the nautilus knew for sure the giant mantas would never harm her or anyone else.

Overjoyed, the nautilus finally said good-bye and headed home. She could hardly wait to tell the true story about the gentle mantas!

We should never fear what we don't know.

The Complaining Cowry

One day four tiger cowries met for lunch along a stretch of bright orange tube-coral reef. In the distance, dolphins frolicked and humpback whales spouted white misty fountains.

"How is everyone?" asked the first cowry, cheerfully.

"Great!" replied the second.

"Terrific!" chimed the third.

"Terrible," grumbled the fourth cowry. "Absolutely rotten. Everything has gone wrong. First, I had to scrub my shell this morning. Then I got lost." He paused to take a bite of his lunch. "Ack! This algae tastes terrible! Why are we eating here?"

"The food is plentiful," explained the first tiger cowry, patiently.

"Well, if you want to gorge yourself, I suppose this place is all right. But this algae is so bitter. I don't see how they can even call this food. And look at all the clumps of sand stuck in here. What kind of a buffet is this? I can't remember when we had such a bad batch."

"Why don't you try this patch over here?" suggested one of the other cowries, motioning to another area.

"Yuck, this algae's even worse. It's so tough. Who wants to chew and chew?"

The other three cowries fell silent. Then they began hurrying away.

The fourth cowry continued to complain, moving in circles as he ate. "This algae must be glued to the rocks. It's so hard to scrape off. Really, it's awful—no, *dreadful* is a better word. Why, this stuff isn't even fit for crabs. And you know, crabs will eat anything. They're such scavengers," the cowry muttered. "We should find another place to eat."

Hearing no reply, the cowry suddenly looked up and noticed his friends had left. He spotted them far away. "Guys . . . hey, guys! Wait for me!"

Complainers may be moving but they're going nowhere.

The Sand Castle

"Son, did you complete your chore?" the father parrotfish asked his young son, who hovered above a patch of coral reef.

"Yes, Father, I did." Moving his fins faster, he hoped his father wouldn't notice the untouched coral beneath the swirling water.

"Son…"

"Well, I'm almost positive I did. Then again, maybe I didn't." Sighing, the youth finally confessed: "I haven't chewed any coral yet, Dad."

"Then it's time to complete your chore. It's important to be responsible."

22

"Okay, okay." The young parrotfish began crunching with his strong beak-like mouth. With each bite, his turquoise and emerald colors shimmered.

"Son, doing your chores is very important. But it's even more important to tell the truth."

"It was only a little lie. It won't harm anyone else," his son answered between bites.

"Little lies quickly become big problems. Others can be hurt if you don't tell the truth."

"What do you mean, Dad?"

"As we chew the coral, we break it down into sand, which provides homes for some and protects the reef for others. Even the children who play on the beach depend upon us. Without us, they wouldn't be able to build those wonderful sand castles we admire so much!"

The young parrotfish took another bite, slowly crunching the coral. He hadn't thought about the possibility of his lie harming others.

Looking toward the shore, he watched busy sand dabs burrowing near the shore break. Tiny brown and silver fish darted in and out of the swaying seaweed, playing tag. Black sea urchins and sea stars bloomed on the reef that was anchored by sand. Laughing happily, children on the beach scooped up bucket after bucket of sand, forming huge sand castles, just out of the reach of the breaking waves.

A lie is like a sand castle;
the first wave of truth will knock it down.

The Flounder's Vision

A baby flounder edged her way into a group of young wrasses, moorish idols, angel, pipe, and goatfishes playing hide-and-seek. "Can I play?"

"Sure, come join us!"

"One, two, three, four, five, six, seven, eight, nine, ten! Ready or not, here we come!" the fishes chorused as they set out to find the pipefish.

With eyes on either side of her body, the little flounder searched right and left. Her plump body followed in the wake of the others.

"I found her!" shouted the moorish idol, pointing to the pipefish, who was hiding upright in the seaweed. "Over here!" With his long, wavy fins, he summoned the others.

"Shucks." The pipefish thought her camouflage had been perfect with her slender body swaying like a strand of seaweed. "Whose turn is it to hide now?"

"Mine," replied the goatfish as she swam off.

Even though the others always found
the hiding fish first, the flounder
enjoyed playing with her friends.

Over the next few weeks, the flounder
began changing. Her right eye moved
toward the left side of her body.
Then the flounder felt herself leaning onto
her right side. No longer upright like the others,
she found herself flattening out and
sinking toward the sandy ocean bottom.
For now, she didn't feel like playing hide-and-seek.

Months later the flounder decided to rejoin the others and play again. By now her transformation was complete. Her right eye had finished traveling, stopping close to her left eye. The flounder's flat, sand-colored body hovered just above the ocean floor like a piece of floating carpet.

"Can I play?" asked the flounder, edging closer to the group.

"Is that you, Flounder? You look different." The fishes stared at the flounder, hardly recognizing their old friend.

"Yes, it's me. I've changed but it's still me."

"What happened to your eyes? They're both on top of what used to be your side. Can you see?" asked the saddle wrasse.

"Oh, I can see fine. In fact, I can see better than before."

"But how can you see to the right and left? Don't you miss half of everything?"

Not giving her a chance to respond, the wrasse turned to the others. "I don't think Flounder should play. She can't possibly see well enough."

"I can *too!*" the flounder countered.

"Okay, Flounder. You can play if you want to," answered the moorish idol. He wasn't so sure she would be able to see very well either but she should be given a chance.

As the others scattered to find the hiding fish, the flounder skimmed along the bottom of the ocean, her eyes searching upward.

I'm going to be the first to find Angelfish. That will show Wrasse and everyone else that I can see just fine! the flounder thought to herself, determined.

Suddenly a dark shadow circled high above the reef, spiraling downward. The flounder's eyes scanned the streamlined shape from below. Busy looking sideways for the angelfish, no one else noticed the danger approaching from above.

"Shark alert!" the flounder yelled out to the others.

Quickly the fishes disappeared into their special hiding places in the reef while the flounder buried herself in the sand. The shadow circled once more and then moved on.

"It's safe now. The shark's gone," the flounder announced, shaking sand off her flat body.

"Looks like I owe you an apology," the wrasse said humbly, coming out of his hiding place. "You saw the shark in time to save us. You **can** see just fine even if both of your eyes are on top."

"Apology accepted, my friend," the flounder replied graciously as she winked an eye.

A different point of view can often help you to see better.

The 'Opihi's Strength

"Today, children, we'll venture to the water's edge," the father 'opihi told his five children. Lined up in a row, they formed a small string of tiny gray striped volcanoes along the top of the rocks, not far from the breakwater.

"Fasten yourselves to the rocks just below the tide's edge. When the ocean recedes, continue to hold on until the waves return."

"How long will that be?"

"Usually, it's just a few hours."

"What if we get tired, Daddy? Or scared?"

"Or hungry?" The littlest one always thought about food.

"The tide must reach its lowest point before it returns. But it always returns. The most important thing to remember is to hold on. No matter what happens, you must never let go."

Little did the father 'opihi know that a large storm was quickly approaching. Before the father could get his family firmly situated on the rocks, the storm's dark clouds blotted out the warm sun. Unleashing its fury, the storm sent waves crashing with great might against the rocks, dislodging crabs and fish from their safe resting places.

"Quick, children, attach yourself to the rocks and don't let go!" the father shouted as the first wave crashed over them. After that, only the pounding of the surf could be heard.

Wave after wave crashed upon the shore with tremendous force and energy. The ocean and the sky twisted together, forming one large silver-gray mass that churned everything in its path.

By morning, the turbulent waves gradually subsided. The ocean regained its shining smooth surface. Thick, dark clouds dispersed before the brilliant light of the sun. Debris lay strewn on the rocks and along the beach. Uprooted trees bobbed in the water. As the tide receded, there was the 'opihi family still firmly fastened to the rocks, safe and sound!

Hold on, no matter how rough the waves.

The Baby Cuttle

One day, a mother squid and a mother cuttle happened to lay their eggs on opposite sides of the same reef. In time, the eggs hatched and the babies grew. The missile-shaped squids darted about on one side of the reef, startling fish and crabs with their swiftness. On the other side, gently waving their clear fins, cuttles peacefully propelled themselves through the water.

Several weeks later one of the baby cuttles swam across the reef and found himself right in the middle of a large gang of squid.

"Hey, what do you want here?" snarled one of the squids, approaching the little cuttle in a menacing manner.

"I was just going—" the baby cuttle attempted to explain.

"Scram! Beat it, flat face. You're not wanted here." Moving closer, the squid threatened the little cuttle with his strong tentacles.

"Yeah, shrimp, leave!" another commanded.

"Look at the clown!" a third squid teased, pointing to the cuttle's rapidly changing colors. The cuttle blushed, changing from gold to brown to silver even more quickly.

"Leave him alone!" commanded a hidden voice.

Everyone turned, only to see the water filling with billowing clouds of black ink.

"Hey, I can't see!" yelped one of the squids.

"Let's get out of here!" shouted another.

In a few minutes the water cleared and the cuttle found an octopus hovering nearby.

"Are you all right?"

"Yes, just a bit scared," answered the little cuttle, trembling.

"Don't worry. They won't be back."

"Why are they mean to me?"

"Name-calling makes them feel powerful," answered the octopus, putting a comforting arm around the young cuttle. "They call me a coward because I won't fight them. It doesn't upset me because I know I'm not afraid of them."

"I don't want to fight them either."

"One day they'll realize how hurtful it is to call names and they'll see that they're actually hurting themselves. Labels, especially nasty ones, aren't nice. Don't worry about what others call you. You're not a clown or a shrimp. Be proud of who you are."

The young cuttle looked up at his new friend and knew he was right. Those squids could call him whatever names they wanted. If the labels weren't true, it didn't matter. As long as he knew who he was, nothing else mattered.

Name callers give themselves a bad name.

The Sea's Treasures

"I have more than you!" shouted a sea star, pointing to his huge pile of mussels.

"Yeah, but mine are bigger!" replied his younger brother.

"It's how many you have that counts!" the sea star argued.

Seeking quiet from her squabbling brothers, their little sister slipped away to the other side of the reef. There she discovered a beautiful bay. Brilliant shades of aquamarine, turquoise, and sapphire shimmered in the sunlight. Bright blue ocean waves capped with pearly foam rolled gently to the shore. Perched on an endless coral bed were many mussels. Sheltered and protected, the bay was a serene haven.

Each day the young sea star admired the many riches offered by the ocean. She delighted in watching the golden plovers dance near the breaking waves and curtsey to the sea foam. Schools of small fish flashed their silver color near the water's edge, followed by a chorus of "Good morning!"

Sometimes, a large green sea turtle would gently poke its head above the water and then, with a flap of its flipper, dive below the surface. Delighted, the sea star would wave back with one of her five friendly arms.

Beyond the reef, the ocean deepened into a dark, almost midnight-blue color, cloaking the marvels of the deep. *What breath-taking mysteries await there?* the sea star wondered.

"If only my foolish brothers could appreciate this. Then they would understand what really counts!" remarked the sea star wistfully. "You have to treasure whatever the sea offers."

34

As she dined on mussels, the sea star remembered to take only what she needed. After each meal, she never forgot to thank the ocean for generously parting with its riches.

From sunrise to sunset, the sea star cherished each gift from the ocean, whether it was the beauty of the moment or a tasty morsel.

"It doesn't matter how much you have or who has more. What matters is whether you're happy with what you have," the sea star murmured contentedly as she watched the sun set, pouring its golden light into the serene ocean.

Contentment is by far the best measure of wealth.

35

Crustaceans, Sea Jellies, and Echinoderms

Banded Coral Shrimp

Reef walkers are often greeted by this tiny, colorful shrimp. With distinctive red-and-white stripes, it's also known as the barber-pole shrimp or prawn. Found in tropical seas all over the world, it lives in tide pools or deeper waters near reefs. Reaching two inches in length, this shrimp cleans off parasites from eels and fishes with its pincers. It has five pairs of legs and three pairs of pincers.

36

Hermit Crab

Unlike other crabs completely encased in shells, a hermit crab has no hard shell covering its soft abdomen. To protect itself, the hermit crab lives in a borrowed shell. When the crab outgrows its home, it must search for a larger one. Occasionally hermit crabs have been seen pulling out another crab from a desirable shell. When attacked, the crab uses its enlarged pincer to block the entrance to its shell.

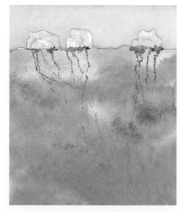

Portuguese Man-of-war

The Portuguese man-of-war is one of about three thousand kinds of sea jellies. Its long blue tentacles hang from a clear float and deliver a very painful sting. While the Portuguese man-of-war looks and acts like a single animal, it's really a colony of animals joined together. Some of the animals catch food by stinging it. Others digest the food, while others lay eggs and produce new animals for the colony.

Sea Star

Although it is sometimes called a starfish, the sea star isn't a fish. Instead it belongs to a group of spiny-skinned animals called *echinoderms,* which also includes sea urchins and sea cucumbers. In addition to tough skins, echinoderms have five rays or arms. If an arm is lost, the sea star can grow another one. Its digestive system extends into each of its arms. Sea stars range in size from an inch to nearly three feet.

Flounder

When first born, this fish looks like most other fishes, swimming upright with an eye positioned on either side of its head. But within two weeks, one of its eyes begins to travel to the other side of its head until both eyes are on the same side. Then the flounder's body flattens. Both eyes are now on its "top" side. This incredible transformation takes approximately four months. In Hawai'i there are thirteen species of righteye and lefteye flounders; lefteye flounders are more common

Manta Ray

These giant creatures, once known as "devilfish" because of their horns, are actually gentle and docile. Cousins to the sharks, mantas feed on plankton and larval fish. Their wingspans can reach up to twenty feet and they can weigh up to 3,000 pounds, making them one of the largest fish.

Moray Eel

The majority of eels found in Hawai'i are the morays, of which there are over thirty-eight species. Most remain hidden in reef crevices their entire lives, feeding on fish, octopus, and crustaceans. The larger moray eels may reach a length of six feet, but most don't exceed two feet. With its mouth gaping open, exposing its sharp teeth, and pulsing rhythmically, the moray eel looks ferocious. However, it's actually pumping water over its gills to breathe oxygen. In early Hawai'i, moray eels were considered spirits or *'amakua.*

Parrotfish

With their strong beaks, the iridescent parrotfishes are considered to be major producers of the world's coral sand. Using its teeth, the fish scrapes algae from coral. Often the parrotfish bites off chunks of coral as it eats the algae. Special bones in its throat grind the coral into fine sand. Parrotfishes vary in color and size with some reaching up to four hundred pounds. Seven species of parrotfish live in the Hawaiian reefs and are collectively known as *uhu.*

Mollusks

Cowry

Prized for its glossy and beautifully colored, oval-shaped shell, the cowry is found in tropical waters. The shell is actually its skeleton and is often covered by a large muscle called a mantle. Secretions from the mantle keep the cowry's shell polished and glistening. The tiger cowry, one of eight known native species, reaches its greatest size in Hawaiian waters.

Cuttle

Looking like a squat squid, thin fins run along the sides of the cuttle. Eight arms and two long tentacles emerge from its head, with the tentacles usually kept retracted in a pouch beneath its eyes. Most cuttles don't exceed one foot in length. Known as "quick-change artists," their skins change color and pattern at an amazing speed, which scientists believe can hypnotize prey, communicate with other cuttles, or create camouflage for protection.

Nautilus

The first relatives of the nautilus appeared 500 million years ago. The six surviving species are little changed, earning them the nickname "living fossil." With many tentacles waving near its eyes and distinctive markings on its spiral shell, the nautilus lives in the deep, primarily at depths of 600 to 800 feet, and swims by using jet propulsion. At night, the nautilus swims closer to the surface to feed. As it grows, the nautilus adds chambers to its shell. They are found off the coasts of Australia, Philippines, New Guinea, Solomon Islands, Fiji, Samoa, and Palau.

Octopus

The curious and intelligent octopus has no skeleton, allowing it to be extremely fluid in its movements and giving it the ability to disappear through small openings. Peering over rocks without giving away its position, it raises its eyes above its body like a periscope. When threatened, the octopus squirts ink to escape. If it loses one of its eight arms, it can grow a new one. An octopus can propel itself through the water, but it prefers to crawl along the ocean floor when looking for food. In Hawaiian, the octopus is called *he'e,* which means to flee or slide along.

38

'Opihi

The *'opihi* or limpet, a primitive snail found along seashores throughout the world, has a flattened, cone-shaped shell. Some live underwater attached to pebbles, stones, or plants. However, most live on rocks between high and low tide levels. When the tide goes out, the *'opihi* remains in the same spot. In heavy surf, the *'opihi* pulls its shell down. With its strong foot, it grips the rock tightly, becoming almost impossible to dislodge.

Squid

By inhaling water, the squid stretches the muscles of its mantle. When the muscles contract, water is squeezed through, allowing the squid to propel itself forward with very little resistance. With its streamlined shape, it speeds through the water like a missile. Over 375 species of squid live in a wide diversity of habitats. They range in size from less than an inch to over 70 feet long. Most squid are aggressive predators. In Hawaiian, it is called *mu he'e*, which means changeable and unsteady, referring to its movements.

39

Seabirds

'Iwa

With a wingspan of over seven feet, the *'iwa* or great frigate bird is one of the larger seabirds in the Pacific region. It is a graceful flier, often seen soaring on long, black angular wings far out at sea. The male has a bright red throat pouch that it inflates like a balloon during mating season. Because it steals fish from other birds, the frigate bird is also known as the *'iwa*, which in Hawaiian means "thief".

Red-Footed Booby

Known for its plunging dives from great heights to catch food, the red-footed booby has distinctive colorings: bright red feet, a blue bill, and a blue face patch. Unlike other boobies, the red-footed booby nests in bushes and low trees and lays only a single egg. When hatched, the chick's skin is black but white down soon protects it. The red-footed booby makes funny grunting sounds, shouts, and whistling noises.

Wedge-Tailed Shearwater

The shearwater skims the surface of the sea or shears the waves, giving rise to its name. The wedge-tailed shearwater gets its particular name from the shape of its fan-like tail. Although an excellent and graceful flier, the shearwater doesn't walk on land but always sits and can often be heard moaning, groaning, or wailing.

About *Fables from the Sea*

Growing up in Wahiawā, Leslie's dream was to write and illustrate books with Kathleen, her childhood friend. Their first book, the award-winning *Fables from the Garden,* is a true gift of friendship and the fulfillment of a promise made in the first grade. With *Fables from the Sea,* their friendship and dreams continue.

About the Author

A graduate of Leilehua High School, Leslie Ann Hayashi received her Bachelor of Arts with distinction from Stanford University and her Juris Doctor degree from Georgetown University Law Center. She currently serves as a district court judge in Honolulu, where she resides with her husband Alan Van Etten and their two young sons, Justin and Taylor. Her "Thoughts for a Dead Japanese Fisherman" was the 1995 Grand Prize Winner in the *Honolulu Magazine* / Borders Books and Music fiction contest. Even before she met her childhood friend, Kathleen Wong, in the first grade, Leslie knew she wanted to be a writer.

About the Illustrator

Kathleen Wong Bishop is a graduate of Roosevelt High School and Stanford University. She now resides in Phoenix, Arizona, with her husband David and their three children, Lisa, Daniel, and Rachel. Caring for her family brings her much joy. She has been a city planner, a community activist, and an educator and is excited to launch her new career as an artist—a talent only recently discovered as a result of Leslie's dream to write. Kathleen has taught Sunday School for many years and is currently the Christian Education Coordinator at Shepherd of the Hills Church. She also enjoys helping people explore their spirituality through creative activities.

Kathleen Wong Bishop and Leslie Ann Hayashi

Photograph by Jennifer Crites